T0063255

The Castle
of the Dead

Jayson Pauley

AuthorHouse™ LLC
1663 Liberty Drive
Bloomington, IN 47403
www.authorhouse.com
Phone: 1-800-839-8640

Published by AuthorHouse   08/25/2014

ISBN: 978-1-4969-3630-1 (sc)
ISBN: 978-1-4969-3644-8 (e)

Chapter One

Welcome To the Castle of the Dead

The stars were shining brightly in the clear night sky, with the full moon hovering, watching, and illuminating everything. Voices could be heard in the distance as a young knight slowly trotted along on his horse companion, paying no mind to the voices. The voices started to become more distinct as the knight was getting closer to the forest. *"That poor gentleman was hysterical and speaking unintelligible things after they found him wondering near that horrific forest,"* one voice said as if having a conversation. The knight came to a stop as the second distinct voice spoke. *"For what would drive a person to enter the forest and venture towards that cursed castle is beyond insanity. That land has been condemned by evil for over ten years now."* The knight could not find where the voices were coming from and shrugged it off as being part of the haunted land into which he ventured. He continued on the path leading to the forest about which the mysterious voices talked.

The clouds became dark, black as the heart of Satan as the brave adventurer entered the forest, riding his noble steed towards the mysterious castle buried deep in the treacherous soul of the haunted forest. This place was deemed *The Castle of the Dead*. It is known in far off lands that if any man, woman or child dares to enter this forsaken place, their souls shall be tortured and devoured by whatever evil that lays within.

The forest was dense, claustrophobic, with dead tree branches reaching out to the path, trying to claim another victim. No signs of life could be seen, as all the trees were dried and decayed, yet they were still living. The knight rubbed the back of his horse's neck to calm it down. He could not afford to be knocked off and stranded in the middle of this forsaken place. As he traveled the narrow path, he glanced side to side, looking for anything that could prove to him that the forest was haunted. Coming from an honorable kingdom, and raised not to believe in such evils, he wanted to know if such things could exist. The trees looked more like horrific creatures to the knight than actual dried up trees. So the knight knew that such evils might exist if a forest could be shaped like this. The road to hell is usually paved with good intentions, but he was determined to discover the truth about this land.

His armor had a faint glow from the beams of light cast through the clouds from the moon as he broke the plain of the forest. The steed that he rode upon was blackish--a slight crimson glow that seemed out of place--and had chain mail armor with symbols marking the knight's kingdom. The clouds began to dig their claws into the moon, casting an eerie dark liquid shadow upon the land. The glow from the knight's armor faded like a candle smothered with a dark cloth, yet the crimson glow around his steed remained. As the noble cavalier slowly stopped near the castle gate, the wind howled like a pack of wolves stalking their prey. The knight's steed reared up from this high-pitched howl, knocking its rider to the ground with a hard thud of metal and stone. As his steed ran off, the capable knight rose to his feet, slightly brushing some of the dirt from his armor, and stood, peering at the castle with a determined look upon his face.

The wind stopped: silence -- not even the whisper of a sound as the knight took a few steps towards the castle. The temperature began to drop drastically as he took a couple more steps. A soft sound of metal rattling, like a rattlesnake ready to strike its victim, began to ring in the knight's ears. His body was shaking uncontrollably from the drop in temperature, yet he couldn't feel the cold biting at his flesh like a million needles. White puffs of mist began to spray from his helmet--a dragon's nostrils ready to spew fire--each time he exhaled. His misty breath seemed to linger in the air as time almost seemed to be frozen in this place. The courageous knight ignored this, feeling it wasn't important as he walked to the entrance of the courtyard and stopped.

Looking peerlessly at the soulless structure of the castle, where no living person has stepped foot upon in ten years, for the castle was broken and crumbling. It almost looked like the castle was stepped on by a massive creature. How could that be possible, the knight knew nothing of such existed? There were burnt claw marks running across the walls of the towers. Holes were punched out; concrete slabs were laying all over the ground. Walls were knocked over and pushed in, as if something forced its way in. Some areas looked as if something came out from the inside. The feeling the knight felt shivering up his body was that the castle seemed to almost mock him for being a knight. Unsheathing his sword and gripping his shield, he walked bravely, honorably, and full of courage into the maw of the desecrated ruins.

Upon entering the courtyard of the castle, the devoted knight was struck with a gust of wind that held the stench of the dead. This unbearable, putrid and nauseating stench brought him to one knee, immobilizing him for a brief moment. A mass pressure gripped his head with such force that it felt like his head was going to burst like a melon in a vice. Sounds of battle began to fill the knight's ears--screams, the echoes of metal cutting through flesh and clashing with bone, the gurgling sound as someone takes their last breath before the darkness comes. He clawed at his helmet like it was an infected wound, trying to rip it from his flesh, yet to no avail the helmet stayed put. Then the sounds of battle went silent.

Opening his eyes, the unwavering knight noticed the sun was shining, with rays of light beaming through a window high in the wall in front of him. He was no longer standing in front of the castle ruins; he was walking towards the direction of the light, and he was walking between a row of knights and guards on each side of him. Each knight would salute him, "Hail, Captain" as he passed them. As this was happening the confused knight realized he was not in control of himself. It felt as if he was just peering through the eyes of this person. He looked around as much as he could, noticing the room he was in was similar to the throne room in his kingdom. As he got closer to what would be the throne, the light beaming through the window became blinding. Not being in control, he could not shield his eyes. The person he was seeing through didn't seem to notice or be bothered by it.

"Ah, my son, Captain of the guard, has arrived at last." The voice boomed with authority as the light vanished, and the knight could see it was the king speaking. It was his king he was seeing. Yet he could not remember this particular moment. He knew he was the captain of the guard in his kingdom. He knew this was his king speaking. He also knew he was watching this through the eyes of someone else, most likely his own, but could not remember when this had happened. "What news from our estates in the north?" The kings' voice boomed once again with authority. The knight then heard another voice ring in his ears, as if spoken from his own lips, "Soon." But this voice did not sound like the knight's voice, not exactly, it had more of a darker, deeper tone.

As soon as this was spoken, the knight's vision shifted towards the exit where all the guards that were lined up began to march out of the throne room. Then the strange vision vanished.

Struggling to get back to his feet, the undaunted knight glared, shocked at what was all around him. He was looking at mutilated corpses that were not there when he had first stepped foot into the courtyard. Slowly looking around, trying not to make any sudden moves as he gazed wide-eyed at the hundreds of blood-soaked body parts littering the courtyard.

There was an eerie glow coming from the inner curtain walls of the courtyard, like there were torches hanging from the crumbling stone. Yet, there were no torches, no flames, nothing that could illuminate the courtyard with as much light. The glow from the full moon was blanketed from heavy cloud cover that seemed to move like a dark, blackish liquid: oil flowing through water. The courtyard was fairly visible with the glow radiating from the walls. There was what appeared to be a cobblestone pathway leading from the inner gateway through the center of the courtyard. There were stones missing from the path while others were covered in dried blood and dirt. The path appeared to come to an end as it met up with a lonely, dried out, desecrated husk of a tree. The branches were twisted and deformed arms and claws, scooping up and shredding someone to pieces if he inched too close. This demonic looking tree had a full torso with its arms drooping and hanging from its dead, rotten branches. The bottom half of the corpse was laying at the bottom of the tree, like the victim was cut in half before making it to safety in the tree. Dried blood had dyed the tree a darker crimson than its original color. The illumination from the walls was also casting evil shadows throughout the courtyard. Twisted figures of shadows danced a horrific scene around the walls. Some of the shadows appeared to creep out from under the corpses and come to life. They looked as if to mock the living as they moved and existed without anything living to create them. Then the shadows started to fade slowly as the eerie glow dimmed to a dull existence.

Before the steady knight could blink, take a breath or even make any movements to investigate what had happened, the bodies started to rise slowly. They rose up as if they were falling, but falling in reverse, like they were being reborn from their gruesome death. Invisible strings seem to be pulling at each of the bodies' limbs, directing them in some horrific puppet show, to be pieced back together. Legs, arms, and severed heads began to float up off the ground. Blood splatter floated up after the limbs and seeped back into the open wounds as they began to reattach themselves to the correct bodies they belonged to. The blood coating the tree started to drip and rain upwards as it found its home inside the remains resting on the decayed branches. The lower half rose up off the ground and leaped up to the upper torso, re-attaching itself, and becoming whole. Then the tree started to move and shake the full bodily remains free as flat, dark-green leaves started to grow and twist out from the branches. One head laying near the tree began to roll backwards to its correct torso and reattached itself. After it had come together with its body, the arms began to swing violently backwards, pulling itself in reverse. The body leaped up into the air after crawling several feet as its lower half stood up and attached itself to the torso. The uncertain knight stood motionless, like a statue decorating the courtyard. If it was not for the faint sound of his heart beating in his ears, he might have thought he died and gone to hell.

After this astounding event came to its closing, the knight still stood frozen in place, gazing at a sight his brain could not yet fully grasp. The corpses he had previously watched being pieced back together were now regular town folk celebrating some special event. The men were all dressed in fancy tunics while the women were wearing gowns and dresses. The women's dresses were a ray of colors across the rainbow spectrum. One lady had a bright flowing red dress with golden laces across the chest, squishing her breasts up to her neck to make sure her cleavage was showing more than the other women. The knight, still in a frozen state, recognized this lady to possibly be of royalty, maybe a princess. The rest of the women had dresses of many designs with long trains flowing on the ground and slim, elegant gowns with a two piece color patterns. The men were not dressed as fancy as the majority of the women. The color range of tunics was the same as the dresses. Each man matched with the woman they were with, in color and style. Some of the men's tunics had different color patterns stitched in the fabric, with matching buttons down the center of the tunics.

The courtyard was illuminated brighter by real torches hanging from the walls, and torch posts planted in the ground along the cobblestone path. The path was a flourish of colored stones in swirl patterns leading up to and circling a beautifully flourished yew tree. It stood like a wondrous green giant with a reddish mahogany trunk glowing in the torchlight. Its lanceolate, flat leaves were flowing in the breeze like a beautiful woman's hair. Beyond the tree, the cobblestone path continued from its circle around it, leading to the entryway of the castle. The rest of the courtyard was an ocean of green grass, not yet long enough to flow with the wind like ocean waves.

The knight, playing statue from shock and awe stood out amongst the crowd like a village on fire, yet no one noticed or paid any attention to him. He watched the crowd as they were enjoying the festivities and noticed that there were children amongst them. Girls and boys laughing and having a great time with each other, all dressed in the same formal dresses and tunics as the adults.

Getting his emotions back in check, and being further recovered from the trauma of witnessing such a strange event, the stable knight began to walk the courtyard. He noticed that there were no guards around, and possibly having royalty among the festivities. He thought this was very unusual. He walked closer to the archway that would lead into the castle and as he got within a few feet from it, three guards appeared with their swords and shields drawn. Being a fellow knight himself, he tried to communicate with the three guards to find out what the celebration was about. The guards immediately pointed their fingers outward in a shooing motion. The knight turned around slightly to notice one of the townsfolk walking away from where he was standing. The three guards were back in their defensive postures when the knight turned back to face them. They did not even seem to notice he was there. This frustrated him to an extreme extent, so he tried to walk past the guards to see if he could get some reaction from them. As he took a step towards the guards, he came in contact with an invisible barrier that prevented his forward momentum. He felt a strange sensation slither through his body, then the pain of crashing face first into the firm ground. The sound of metal contacting the gravel with an intense impact echoed throughout the courtyard. He strained to pick himself up off the ground with the weight of the armor acting like an anchor dragging him down.

When he finally got back to his feet, standing tall, and peering through his helmet, he noticed that he was back at the entrance to the courtyard. In front of him, he also detected that the courtyard was littered with the decomposing bodies he had seen earlier. The torches were gone and the eerie glow was back. The beautiful yew tree was back to its demonic, mangled form. The ocean of green grass was no longer. In its places was a sea of dirt and dried blood. This caused an unsettling feeling to ripple up through the knight's body. He shook off the feeling and began to walk back into the courtyard. Once he stepped foot in the exact place before, the corpses started to move and play out the same scene he watched previously. The grotesque corpse puppet show performed its encore exactly like before and ended with the townsfolk having their celebration. More confusion than fear fell over the knight from watching the same thing happen twice.

After a few moments passed, the knight began to make his way back through the crowd of townsfolk, back towards the archway leading into the castle. As he walked, he passed by many people laughing, talking, and having a good time, yet he could hear no sounds coming from anywhere or anyone in the courtyard. When he reached the center of the courtyard, next to the yew tree, the three guards came rushing out of the archway as they did before. The knight noticed it was due to a gentleman trying to enter the castle, the same someone he noticed walking away from him when he had previously tried to enter. After the gentleman walked away, the three guards moved from their post and began to walk towards the center of the courtyard. They passed the knight and the yew tree in quick fashion and made their new guarding post the inner gateway of the courtyard. The knight looked back towards the castle entrance and noticed a new person standing next to the archway. The knight noticed that this one was dressed in full black plate, sword, shield, and the same markings as his own he was currently wearing. Then a rush of guards came swarming out of the archway like an angry mob of bees from their disturbed hive. The townsfolk did not seem to be bothered by this and kept to their festivities. The swarm of guards positioned themselves throughout the courtyard, standing ready, waiting for any command.

The knight paid more attention to the person standing next to the archway than the guards. He felt that a horrific event was about to take place and that the command was going to come from this person. In that moment that the feeling struck the core of the knight and bubbled in his gut like frogs trying to escape a cauldron of boiling water, he saw this black knight's arm rise. His hand went up to his neck and made a fist with only his index finger still out. At that very moment, one of the younger children, a dark haired boy wearing a dark blue tunic, went up to one of the guards. Then the black knight gave the command by running that finger across his neck like he was slicing his own throat. The young boy stood motionless as the guard's sword protruded from the back of his neck.

The sounds of battle once again filled the knight's ears as he watched the horrific event. The guards sliced, chopped, and stabbed through body after body. Men, woman, and children screaming and running for their lives were cut down with no remorse. A young girl, barely in the twenty years of her life, began to climb the tree as the knight watched a guard cut through her midsection and separate her torso from her waist. The lower half fell to the ground with a wet thud while her torso bled out all over the tree. Her dead, blank eyes stared at the knight like she was blaming him for this tragedy. The knight looked away just in time to see a gentleman get sliced in half while he tried to run. He was still alive after hitting the red grass, and began to crawl franticly. Then his head was severed, which rolled several feet away from his lifeless torso. The knight could not close his eyes to the massacre around him. He watched as every living person from the festival was reduced to a pile of blood and severed limbs. The sounds of battle and death faded once again. The beautiful ocean of green grass was now a flowing ocean of crimson.

The knight's body finally loosened up from the tension and he dashed as fast as he could for the castle archway. The sound of his armor clanking from that type of movement should have echoed throughout the courtyard, yet no sound was made. His footfalls should have made a horrific squishing and sloshing sound, yet again, no sound came from his movements. He passed up several guards just standing in place looking at the bloodbath before them. They paid him no mind as he rushed passed them. As he got closer to the archway, he finally noticed that the other knight was nowhere to be found, that he must have entered the castle after giving the kill command.

He then suddenly remembered the invisible barrier that prevented him from entering previously and tried to slow his drive before crashing into it. His momentum could not be reduced as he prepared for a painful collision. He hit the area where the barrier was with his shoulder out front, ready to crash through it like a frail wooden door, yet there was no impact, no painful crash, just air being passed through. The knight struck a raised stone step after passing through the archway, which sent him flying several feet before his armor crashed and scraped against the stone floor with a high pitched squeal that tore at his ears. He slid several more feet, cringing from the sound his armor and the stone floor made as they grinded together before the darkness enveloped him.

Chapter Two

Please Stay Awhile

Two young boys walked side by side through a stone corridor leading into a grand room of stone and marble. A giant stained glass window that portrayed a great man, the king, illuminated the boys as they entered the throne room. The floor was a mirror-shined marble with a checker-patterned path leading to a set of five steps that wrapped in half a circle and connected with the back wall. On top of these steps rested a grand chair of gold, silver, and a variety of gems encrusted in the base and arm rests. The boys looked at each other and smiled as they took a step forward and collided with something in front of them. They both looked to see that someone was now standing in front of them, and when they peered up to see who it was, a look of horror washed over their faces. It was the king, but something was wrong with his face, but worst of all, there was a sword embedded in his chest.

The knight woke up with a fright, quickly looking around trying to remember where he was. There was nothing but pitch-black darkness all around the knight as he picked himself up off the hard stone floor. He noticed the weight of his gear was off; that his sword and shield were no longer with him. He felt around his armor to make sure. No sheath, no sword, and no shield were on his person. He then started to turn around or felt himself turn around, not knowing which due to the darkness surrounding him. He noticed a bright light emanating from a room in the distance from where he felt himself standing. Either the light did not seem strong enough to penetrate the dark, or the darkness was so strong it warded off all light. He could not tell, so he lined himself up with it, and walked very slowly towards it. The knight felt his body move forward at an increased rate, like many hands were placed on his back and were pushing him forward. He could feel the tingling in his body as his feet stayed still, yet his body moved closer and closer to the lighted doorway. The light seemed to be moving at an increased rate as well, like it was being pushed or pulled closer to him. It felt like he was in a jousting competition with the light source, and a collision was imminent with nothing to defend himself with. The impact was coming at an accelerated rate, so the knight clenched his fists and placed them in front of his helmet. He clamped his arms together, wrist to wrist, and elbow to elbow to act as a shield to protect his face and neck, a natural human instinct. He knew he was fully armored in plate and his face would be protected by his helmet, but the human defensive instinct was too strong for him to ignore. He closed his eyes and clenched his body tightly as the light engulfed him.

The knight felt nothing as an illumination of light was penetrating through his eyelids. His body felt still, no forward momentum, no strange feeling of many hands all over him, and most of all, no pain. His muscles let go of the tension, and he lowered his arms down to his sides. His heart slowed its erratic beat and came to a calm as he opened his eyes slowly, letting them adjust to the brightness of his surroundings. What the knight saw was the most extravagant, grand, and luxurious room he had ever seen. This room was untouched by the decay the rest of the castle had been affected by. Not one speck of dust desecrated the magnificence of what this room stood for. The throne room was still shining and reflecting light like a thousand diamonds in the radiance of the sun.

There was a grand stained glass window illuminating the room from the back center wall. This window portrayed an older man wearing a grand crown and an elegant robe. The knight knew it was the castle's king. Underneath the window was the king's throne. This magnificent chair was all black with gold linings running through the arms and back. The cushions on the back and the seat were a crimson red with golden threads creating a swirl pattern throughout the fabric. The back of the chair had, what appeared to the knight as spines splitting from the rest of the chair. It made the chair seem like it had claws and on the tip of these claws rested small golden cylinders with a diamond resting on each one. The golden linings ran spiral around each of the spines to the golden cylinders. When looked at, the gold seems to flow from the cylinders down through each piece of the chair and end at the base pattern that mimics a moving river of gold. The throne sat on top of the marble stairs. Five steps leading down to a platform step that could be walked along, then four more steps leading the grand marble floor. A checkered pattern path with a white outline lead from the steps to the entrance of the room. The rest of the floor was a black marble finish. The whole floor shined and acted like a giant mirror reflecting images of the whole room.

The knight stepped forward a few paces and looked around the grand room. There were two corridors, one on each side of the steps leading to the king's throne. The steps stretched the whole middle wall, extending from it in a half circle. There were torch cradles mounted on each side of the archways of the corridors. The lit torches resting in them helped add a complementary light radiance to the room. Hanging from the high stone ceiling was a silver and golden chandelier that had thirteen pearl white candles in gem-encrusted holders on the outer ring. There were eight brace bars connecting the outer ring with the inner ring. This inner ring had four silver chains holding it to an upper ring that had a golden-lined silver cross in the middle of it. Each of the chains were attached to one of the four ends of the cross, which was connected to the main chain that ran up to its connecting point in the stone ceiling. The candles burned with a bright, radiant light that finished the full illumination of the magnificent throne room.

Getting a closer look around the whole room, from top to bottom, the knight began to walk towards the throne. Each one of his steps echoed a metallic sound throughout the room, as if a blacksmith was pounding out the finishing touches of his creation. Looking down at his feet as his metal boots clanged with the marble floor, he noticed that the whole room was reflecting off its mirror shine, except he had no reflection. He stopped and stared at the floor like he was trying to make himself reflect, trying to understand why he was denied a reflection.

As he peered into the reflected throne room, a single drop of crimson blood splashed on the marble floor. The blood splatter had a small hint of steam resonating from it as the marble began to deteriorate. Another drop splashed down next to the first, then another, and another. Each splash began to eat away at the marble floor like an acid. Then a downpour of blood pelted the marble floor, the steps leading to the throne, and the throne itself. The walls were running with blood and as the blood slithered down the walls, a decade and desecrated version was appearing. The knight looked at the ceiling to see where the blood might be coming from. To his surprise, it was the ceiling itself. It was decaying in a rain of blood, leaving behind a withered and torn remains. The entire throne room was bleeding itself out and leaving behind a ruined, desolate, cracked and broken version of its once magnificent glory. The chain holding the chandelier was cracking and hissing as the blood decay ate away at it. Then it finally let go, snapping, and crashing to the floor with a thunderous sound that echoed and reverberated off every wall. A spider web cracked indent in the marble spread through the floor as the chandelier came to its final resting place. The knight gazed at the throne. This once magnificent, gloriously designed chair that represented a seat of power, now represented decay and death. The seat cushions were shredded and lacked the beauty of its once crimson color. The gold trimmings were dull and colorless, lacking the beauty and symbolism they once held.

The knight gazed with clearer vision as the once radiant throne room transformed into a bleak, dreary, rotten, and broken version of itself. He also began to notice that the blood that rained down was now forming a pool directly in front of the steps leading to the throne. The perfect circular pool of blood had no base which to hold it in, yet it stayed as if it was contained within something that could not be seen. Walking ever cautiously around the broken and shattered chandelier, the knight sought a closer look at this mysterious pool of dark crimson blood. As he stepped closer to the dark liquid, it began to ripple and bubble in the middle, like someone was drowning under the horrific watery fluid. Then the pool began to slither itself up the ruined steps and engulfed the throne. The knight watched as a figure began to form out from the crimson liquid. A decayed skeletal figure, with ragged and rotten clothes, merged as the crimson moved slightly back.

Sitting upon his throne once again was the king, yet rotten and withered with a cracked and beaten crown. The knight stepped up one step to the throne, and as he did, the crimson ooze began to ripple. He went up to the second step out of curiosity, and again the crimson rippled, with more force. Walking up to the third step, the crimson rippled violently, then splashed into the king's decayed body. It began to seep into every inch of the king's body, turning muscle tissue pink and red. Veins started to pulsate as blood flowed through them. Skin began to scab up at a rapid pace and then heal into a light flesh tone.

The knight, once again played statue, amazed and frightened at what he had just witnessed.

Faster than the knight could blink, the king's body was now standing directly in front of him, face to face with hard, cold eyes staring him down. The king was in full royal dress, as if he had never died. His crown had a full mirror shine and radiance from it that the knight could see his reflection perfectly. Dressed only in basic cotton tunic and leggings that go underneath a knight or soldier's armor, he realized that his protective armor was gone. The king raised his arm, and as it came above the knight's left shoulder, he realized that the king was pointing at something behind him. Before he turned around, he also noticed that the king's mouth began to move in an aggressive manner, like he was yelling out something. Yet, no sound was heard.

Pivoting his feet as he began to turn around, the knight saw, to his surprise, a battle happening between that king's royal guards and the familiar black knight that was in the courtyard giving the kill command to the other guards. The sounds of battle began to echo in the knight's ears as they did before.

"What is the meaning…" The voice faded into the background as the sounds of swords clashed against each other.

"Do you realize…" Again the voice drifted into the echoing of the swords meeting with great force.

The knight watched the battle ensue as the vicious black knight slayed each guard one-by-one. The battle was over and the knight knew this as only two guards remained, tired and fearful in their stance. The wicked black knight lunged towards the remaining guards. The sounds of their battle echoed throughout the throne room. Each clash of swords reverberated sound waves that seem to alter the appearance of the room, from its decayed version back to its perfect version, then back again. The knight noticed that each time the room changed its state of being, there was an after image of a silhouette hovering over the villainous black knight. This silhouette was bigger than any man that the knight knew had existed. It did not appear to be or feel like anything from the living realm. A cold feeling shivered throughout the knight's body as he watched the last two of the royal guard parish at the end of a sword.

As soon as the last of the guard's bodies hit the floor, a woman came running in through a side room. She stopped dead in her tracks as she noticed the massacre in front of her. She was wearing a long red dress that had golden lace throughout it. Long flowing brown hair swayed across her shoulders as she stood motionless, terror-stricken, with a look of fright covering her face. As petrified as the woman was, she was still magnificent in her beauty. A radiant glow resonated from her that captivated any man who caught a glimpse of her. The knight stared at her for a moment and realized that this woman was the one he saw at the celebration, the one he knew who looked like royalty.

The king turned to the woman and waved his arm in a violent, shooing motion while his lips moved, screaming something at her that could not be heard. The devilish black knight glared at the king, then at the woman. She glared back at him, then darted for the king, disobeying this order. The black knight noticed that she was not heading directly to the king; she was going for one of the swords on the floor that belonged to one of the dead guards. Being well trained in combat and fighting techniques from her child years to young adulthood, she knew if she got the sword, she could protect the king. Knowing that she was a skilled fighter, the foul black knight knew he had to react fast to keep her away from the sword and the king. He honed in on her movement, grabbed the hilt of his sword with both hands, raising it above his head. Then he lunged forward, bringing his arms down in a fast, powerful motion. He let the sword go at the right time and angle so it moved in a downward trajectory towards the woman.

The sword spun hilt over tip, hilt over tip as it traveled the short distance between the black knight and the woman. Time slowed down as the knight watched the sword make its way closer to the woman. Leaping in front of the sword, the knight thought he could somehow save the woman's life, yet to no avail, the sword past right through him as if he was not even there. The tip of the blade then made its way to the woman's right thigh and began to push itself through her flesh. The blade tip exited through the other side of her thigh and continued its momentum. The impact started to buckle her right leg slowly out from under her.

The king watched in torment as the hilt of the sword smashed into her thigh, bringing her leg up underneath her. Her body slowly twisted to the right as she hovered a few inches from the floor. Time sped back up to its normal state as the woman crashed hard onto the floor. A cry of pain boomed and echoed throughout the whole throne room, so horrific and agonizing that the knight covered his ears and shivered in fear.

The woman was a fighter, and she knew she still had fight left in her. Even though the sword was still buried deep in her leg, she sucked in a deep breath and pushed through the pain as she tried to get up off the floor. The vile black knight saw her determination and knew she would never give up, so he burst into a sprint to prevent her from getting up and getting to the sword. The dark silhouette grew bigger, as the black knight closed his distance, and as he got closer, a shadowy arm swooped across the room and shoved the knight, still shaken up from the loud shriek, across the room and into the wall. The impact knocked the breath out of him and shook him out of his fearful state. Taking a brief moment to get his senses back, the knight looked up with semi-blurry vision towards the center room, to see that the damnable black knight had gotten to the woman. The king was on his knees and looked like he was begging and pleading for the woman's life. The knight knew he was unable to do anything to prevent what was about to happen, and was forced to watch what he felt to be a horrific event.

Grabbing the hilt of the sword, the sinister black knight held the woman down with his left leg and began to pull the sword from her leg slowly. No sounds could be heard as the woman's face showed her screaming in agony. The sword was half sticking out on both sides of her thigh when he started to press down on the hilt, forcing the blade to come up, cutting more into her flesh. Lifting his left leg up off her, he slammed it down onto the hilt of the sword with great force that it sliced through her leg completely, leaving it attached by a piece of skin and tissue. The room then thundered and echoed once again with a horrific, torturous scream of pain. A scream that would have the power to wake the dead and have them shivering in their coffins. Still sitting against the wall, the knight covered his ears but could not look away. The king just slumped down and wept, helpless and broken, unable to do anything.

Being the fighter that she was, the woman started to crawl towards the sword she originally wanted to get. A few more steps and she would have had it. Blood was gushing out of her severed leg as she endured the pain enough to be able to reach the sword. She grabbed the hilt, and as she started to raise it up off the floor, her arm burst into a spray of blood as it was viciously sliced off. Again no sound was made, nor heard, as the woman, clearly in pain, showed signs of a painful scream on her face. The black knight then picked up the sword she had, and with great force and power, he slammed the tip into her other leg. The force was so great that it penetrated all the way through her leg, and buried itself into the marble floor, pinning her leg down. He then walked over to another sword laying on the floor and picked it up. Twirling it in his hand, he strolled back to the woman and the pool of blood in which she was wading. He knew her time was up soon with the blood loss, yet he was not done making her suffer. He grabbed the hilt with a firm grip, with the blade pointed down, and then nailed it into her remaining arm, pinning it to the floor as well.

Her body was sprawled out in the shape of a crooked, broken cross as she slowly bled to death. The color was draining from her face as the heinous black knight looked down at her. Knowing she only had moments to live, he took his original sword, twirled it once and slammed the blade into her throat. Blood gushed out of her mouth as she coughed and wheezed her remaining breaths. Her radiant hazel eyes began to glaze slowly over as she felt the darkness closing in on her. He then twisted the blade, breaking the bones in her neck. The sound echoed with the resonance of a tree branch breaking. Then was drowned out with the sound of her skull crushing underneath his metal, armored boot as he stomped on her face, severing her head.

Walking over to the king, who was sobbing to himself the woman's name, "Catheryn," the black knight grabbed him by his royal garb and yanked him up to his feet. He then dragged the king over to the throne and tossed him violently into the chair.

The knight, still sitting against the wall watched the scene continue to play out, feeling helpless, hopeless, sad, lost, anger for everything he has witnessed. He then peered up, continuing to watch, wondering what could have caused all this to happen. He then got back up to his feet, still with an uneasy, fearful feeling running throughout his body. Taking a few steps closer he noticed that the ominous shadow silhouette began to enlarge and turn in his direction as he got closer. Stopping, he noticed the shadow pause. He then took a couple steps back, and the shadow went back to its original state. Fearing that if he decided to get closer the shadow would attack him again, so he remained standing still, continuing to watch from a distance.

The king coward in his throne, not knowing what the sadistic knight in front of him was going to do. The cold black knight raised his sword tip to the king's chest with his right hand and pressed it against his chest with such force that it made the king scurry back as far as he could in the chair. Then the cruel black knight raised his left hand up to his helmet and slid it off, tossing it to the floor. The king's face went pale with shock, as if he could not believe who the person standing in front of him was.

Squinting and rubbing his eyes, the knight tried to see the face the king was looking at and completely shocked about, yet all the knight could see was a distorted blur of what should be a head and face. He saw that the king's lips started to move, indicating he was talking to the black knight. Something the king said must not have been pleasant because the sword went from his chest to his throat. Then the knight noticed the king's face go pale with fright and his body froze up as if the devil had just walked over his grave. At the same time, the dark shadow silhouette grew bigger and an arm with a demonic looking hand grabbed the king, heaving him up to the ceiling. The ceiling cracked with the force of his body slamming against it, causing a little blood to drop from his mouth. The king stayed pressed against the ceiling; an unseen force from the silhouette was holding him in place. The unyielding black knight then took his sword and placed the hilt on the floor, with the blade tip pointed up and underneath the king. The sword began to rise up slowly, moving towards the king. When it reached the king, his face was trembling in fear with sweat perspiring like he was melting under the sun. The tip of the sword penetrated his chest very slowly, causing his body to start shaking from the pain. With his eyes clenched shut and teeth clamped tightly, he let loose with a silent scream as the blade dug deeper into his flesh. Blood began to drip and rain down from the wound, splashing onto the floor next to the black knight.

The knight watched helplessly as the king was being bled to death, feeling somehow that this was all his fault for coming to this castle. Hearing all the tales and legends he knew he should have never stepped foot in this place, but something compelled him to investigate. His protective armor was gone, his will was broken, and he felt disgraced for feeling so weak and helpless. Yet, through all the hopeless feelings he was experiencing, he started to feel something familiar about the castle and everything that he has witnessed. In this moment of clarity, he noticed the king fall from the ceiling and then get tossed into the throne. The sword was all the way into the king's chest and stuck out from the back of the chair. Then the murderous black knight turned to the knight and began walking towards him. As he got closer, he began to fade away, leaving only the dark silhouette behind.

The dark shadowy mass grew bigger as it crept closer to the knight, engulfing the whole room into darkness. A voice spoke with the hiss of a thousand voices crying out in pain, a voice that could bring any living man to his knees and turn him into a fearful, crying infant. The knight cringed as he heard the voice speak to him.

"We come to this moment once again, Victor, faster than anticipated. Your will is still strong, and some memories remain in that withering body of yours."

Chapter Three

To Uncover the Truth

The name, Victor sent a sensation of remembrance throughout the knight's body, like the feeling of a spider crawling across his skin. The name was his own, and he had forgotten it. The feeling of forgetting one's own name was unsettling to Victor.

The shadowy mass reached out, clamping onto Victor's head with its demonic claws while he was in mid-thought. "Let's see if we can dig deeper into that mind and find out what memories you still cling to."

Being completely engulfed into darkness, Victor felt the sickening feeling of being alone and empty inside wash through his body, like being bathed in the tears of the lost and damned. His heartbeat pulsed slow and hard ripples through his center that weakened him like a broken child, cowering from another beating. A single tear rolled down his face as he dropped to the floor. He closed his eyes and curled up into a fetal position, wishing for death to come take him away from all the pain and suffering.

"Confront your demons son. Never give up during any hardships you face, and you shall always emerge victoriously"

Opening his eyes to the sound of a familiar voice, Victor could see a young man kneeling down in front of a small child, comforting him. The child appeared to have a dark bruise around his left eye. Victor slowly sat up and watched the two figures, who appeared to be inside a kid's bedroom. There was a wooden storage trunk; hand carved resting in front of a small bed made from a beautiful burgundy colored wood. There were a few other decorations and furniture around the room, but Victor paid no mind to them as he was still focused on the child.

"Remember son, you have the power in here," placing his hand on the boy's head, "to overcome any confrontations that may come as you get older."

Victor's memory of this moment came to him like a swift blow to the side of his head. This moment in time was when his father, the king, tried to comfort him when his mother died. That getting into fights with the other children would not make things better, and would not make his mother happy.

Victor stood himself up, and as he did, the memory faded into nothingness, and only an eerie darkness remained. He began to walk forward; arms stretched out to feel his way out of the lack of light. As he crept forward at a slow, cautious pace, he noticed a light source illuminate an archway. As he got closer to the light source, a voice rang out inside his head.

"When are you going to learn that you cannot run from your troubles, of the present, past or even the future?"

Stopping in his tracks, Victor's memory of this moment came to life in front of him as the same room from before appeared. This time the image shown the boy hiding under his bed, and the father trying to coax him out. The boy crawled out. Victor noticed the boy was much older than in the previous memory.

"When will you learn you cannot solve all of your problems with anger?"

Another sharp pain struck Victor as the memory of this moment flooded his brain. He had picked a fight with his brother, even though his brother was stronger and better trained in combat, fought a good fight and lost. Victor's temper was always something easily set off. And the subject matter of this particular fight, and many afterwards was something close to Victor's heart. The girl that Victor was in love with was the girl who was ordained to be his brother's wife. It broke his heart and enraged him every time he would see the two together. Her name was a blur in Victor's mind, and as he struggled to catch her name, the room went dark.

"You will not be king, my son. Your brother is the worthy heir to the throne. He has proven himself a great tactician, to be a great fighter, and most of all

he has control over his emotions. His honor, loyalty, and pride all hold to the highest standers of an heir to the throne. Over the course of these many years, you have faltered in your proving to me that you can be the successor. You are still my son, yet you will not be king."

Victor opened his eyes as moisture streamed down his cheeks. Hearing his father's words ring out, bringing back the pain of that morning where his world shattered in a cataclysmic eruption of rage. He wiped the salt water from his eyes and face, the painful memory still stinging the back of his mind like a relentless scorpion. Standing up, looking around, seeing he was still in the throne room Victor felt an urge to go through the archway that would lead him to the bowels of the castle. Not knowing how much more of the torment he could take from the castle, he stepped forwards to the archway, then descended into the darkness and depth of the lower chambers.

Reaching the last few steps leading to the lower depths of the castle, Victor stepped into the dark room, and in doing so, caused the room to light up in a blinding illumination. Yet, the room was not a room at all, it was a bright green grassy field on a high sunny day. Turning around to see if the steps he just came down were still there, Victor only found more of the same grassy field. He turned back around and felt a cool breeze on his face that made him realize he hadn't felt the sun's rays or the winds breeze in what felt like years. As his ecstasy of this moment came to a high point, the sounds of swords clashing brought him out and back into reality. He looked across the field to his right to find two people sword fighting, but not fighting, more along the lines of training.

Upon getting closer to the two swordfighters, Victor recognized both; one being his brother, the future king, the other being Catheryn, who would be the future queen. Catheryn, the name chimed in Victor's ears with the sound of an angel's harp being played; the heartstrings were plucked, and a peaceful calm fell over Victor. He sat and watched the two swordplay, dodging and parrying each other's attacks with skill and grace. Victor then walked even closer to the vicinity of the two, his eyes focused on Catheryn's movements. As the play-fighting continued, Victor noticed a few flaws in Catheryn's style, which could lead her to getting injured or even killed in a real fight. And then he saw it, the mistake he feared may happen.

Catheryn always had playfulness in her fighting style, since she was a kid being trained by the captain of the guards. She always wanted to be a fighter, even though it was not her role in life, so she had the captain secretly train her. But her intense training never cleared her of her playfulness, and the mistake Victor saw nearly caused her to lose an arm. Her reaction was quick enough to dodge the strike, but the blade still caught her side and sliced into her delicate flesh.

Victor boiled with rage when he heard the scream of agony bellow out from Catheryn, but stayed his ground because he knew he could not do anything. Then he noticed a figure in the distance running towards the two. Victor noticed it was himself from this point in time. When the young Victor reached the two, he punched his brother without hesitation, dropping him to the ground, and then went to aid Catheryn. The image began to distort as young Victor picked Catheryn up and ran towards the castle. The memory faded to complete darkness all around Victor.

Moments Passed in silence and total darkness as Victor stood still, thinking, and reflecting on the memory. He knew that his brother didn't mean to hurt Catheryn, her playfulness is what caused the incident. But his anger always got the best of him, and he didn't realize that he had hit his brother until the confrontation in the castle. Victor also remembered that he had confessed his love to Catheryn while her wound was being sewed up. She told him that she was already tied to his brother emotionally, spiritually, and by rule of the kingdom, and that her feelings would never change. She was flattered that Victor felt that way towards her, but was upset that he would ruin their friendship by wanting more. In this moment, Victor began to realize that this was the turning point, the catalyst that sent him over the edge.

Victor sat in the darkness with a feeling of weakness rippling through his soul. He dropped to his knees, buried his head in his hands, and began to sob. His will to go on was broken. The castle had beaten him, and he was trapped in this hellish place, a prisoner bound never to escape.

"Ah, the Victor I have come to know so well finally reveals himself, broken, beaten, and scared. The anguish is so delicious. I crave more."

Victor knew who was addressing him, but he did not care. The memory of Catheryn not wanting to be a part of his life was too much. Victor did not care for anything in life anymore, and this being that was addressing him knew it.

"Victor, the anguish and pain you radiate is destroying your soul and making you weaker."

A new voice rang out that he knew very well. Catheryn was standing in front of him as he lifted up his head. Victor could not believe that she was actually there. He became so entranced by her that he did not feel the water dripping down his face. The only thing that he could think of at that moment was that, her beauty radiated so much, that the darkness held no ground to its brightness.

The death and destruction that has been around him was nonexistent in her light.

Victor stood up, eyes like a hawk, never leaving Catheryn's form. She was dressed in all white, with her dark brown hair flowing down past her shoulders. Victor did not care at that moment if he fell lifeless. To be within her radiance was as if heaven walked on earth.

"But Victor, you are already dead!" Catheryn's voice exclaimed.

As she spoke, a blood color started to soak through her whole dress ware, till she was fully dressed in crimson. Victor's eyes widened, to the point they could fall out of their sockets. Then Catheryn vanished, speaking her last few words.

"Be strong and noble Victor, and you shall yet save your soul."

He was already broken and beaten causing her words to bounce right off him.

He then began to look around in the midnight void of nothingness as the familiar voice began to torment him once again.

"The time has come Victor, for the truth to be known, and for your soul to be mine. Hell shall reign over the mortal realm once again."

Victor's rage started to boil as a point in the void began to shimmer, like a mirage in the desert. His eyes focused on the image as it was being born, and becoming even clearer. Then the darkness faded and he was standing in the castle courtyard. The castle was not destroyed and in ruins. The courtyard was an ocean of green, and the yew tree in the middle was streaming in the wind, alive and green. Then Victor noticed a great crowd of people flowing into the courtyard from the direction of the common folk's living area. They were all dressed for some celebration.

Victor then noticed a commanding knight in full silver plate and a small platoon of soldier knights. They were alongside guards as they all marched into the courtyard. The leader knight was riding on the back of a black stallion, decorated in protective armor and crests to show he was royalty and in leadership. The knights marched into the castle entrance as the commander dismounted his horse and followed them. The crowd of town's folk was cheering as they all entered the castle.

After the guards and knights faded into the castle, the festivities began. Victor began to remember the previous scene he watched and realized at that moment, he was about to watch it again. As the flashback of the horrific event swept across his mind, he recognized the lead knight as the one who gave the command to kill the town's folk. Yet, this knight was not dressed in black armor. Victor started to walk towards the castle entrance, passing through the town's folk as he did before. He walked into the archway and found himself in the throne room, which he knew was impossible.

As he looked around, he noticed a familiar scene. All the knights and guards were in line formation along the sides of the walkway. The lead knight was standing in front of the king. Victor heard the same familiar voice boom across the room, "Welcome home my son."

He was watching the scene from an outside perspective, and began to remember that this was his welcome home celebration from doing peaceful trade negotiations with three other kingdoms. While watching, Victor wondered why this castle would be haunted with moments of his past. "Soon!" Victor heard his past self's voice ring out, yet it was mixed with a different monotone.

Then he noticed the guards walking out of the throne room, and his past self was walking behind. Victor began to follow, and wondered where this past version of him vanished to, and where the knight in black armor comes in. He knew that black armor was forbidden in any kingdom or for any knight to wear, for it was a symbol of betrayal and the works of evil.

Before Victor could fully exit the throne room, everything went midnight black. Then within that same few seconds, he found himself back outside, in the middle of the celebration. A few moments past when he noticed the guards flowing out of the castle, as they did before. The black knight emerged last. As he did, everything went black once again. When the light was reborn, Victor found himself looking out above the celebration.

He was watching the guards swarm around the courtyard as they did before. He tried to look around but found himself unable to move. Then he felt a small sensation of his arm moving. His eyes were visually focused on the town's folk as the guards began to slaughter them once again.

Victor could feel a boiling rage inside him that was not his own. As the rage grew, he felt himself turn and his vision changed to where he was standing at the entryway to the throne room. He felt helpless as his body began to walk forward. As he got closer to the throne room, the royal guards came charging at him. Victor's normal reaction was to defend himself, but found that he was unable to. Yet, he felt the tingling sensation of his body moving in a defensive stance. Before he realized it, both of the royal guards were dead. He knew that it was him that did it; the feeling was too familiar.

Then Victor watched as he came to the entryway to the throne room, and noticed two hands come up and push open the double doors, that were now closed, to reveal the same throne room as he seen before. This time four of the remaining royal guards charged him. Victor realized this was the scene he had watched before where the black knight came to kill the king.

Victor watched the scene play out as it did before, but from the view of the black knight. The royal guards dropped as they did before, and Catheryn came into the scene. Victor knew what was about to happen, and he began to break down inside, for he knew he was about to watch the woman he loved get butchered once again. An evil, dark rage began to ripple through Victor, but it was not directly from him.

When that happened, Victor watched as Catheryn was taken down with the sword. He listened to every scream that was not heard from the previous event. Each scream reverberated through his body and made his soul cry in pain. Victor's sight never left the body of Catheryn as her limbs were brutally chopped off one by one. Each time the sword struck her body, Victor felt the pain. It became so unbearable that he just wanted to take her place and have his life ended.

"Victor," a familiar, torturous and venomous voice exploded in Victor's ears.

"Why would you want to take her place, when it was you who took her life?"

The realization of all the events finally struck him, like a mace crushing some poor bastard's skull. All the memories came rushing in, wave after wave, like a relentless storm over the ocean. Victor was always jealous of his brother being heir to the throne and Catheryn being his wife. His jealousy and selfishness took control over him and grabbed the attention of a demon that fed off it. This demon came to Victor and offered him everything if he would give himself up willingly. Victor was too blinded with wanting to be king and to have Catheryn as his wife that he agreed to the offer without hesitation and without knowing what was involved.

As all these memories were rushing back, the scene was motionless with Catheryn's body lying, bloody and chopped up in front of him. His body became his own once again. He dropped to both knees with a thunderous clash of metal and marble floor. He cradled the remains of Catheryn's body, as blood was dripping slowly on the floor. He began to cry violently. His body shook, making his armor rattle. He didn't want to believe that he could kill the only thing in his life that he loved, and in such a horrific way.

When his eyes reopened from crying so much, he focused enough to see that her body was gone and that he had blood pools in his palms. As he spread his fingers apart, the blood dripped to the floor. The blood drops formed into rose pedals as they slowly glided downwards. Victor wept once again. The pain of loss was so great, as if the world ended, and he was the only one left. His heaven was gone, and his world destroyed; his light was extinguished and darkness only remained. He knew that the king had also fallen by his hands. His father, murdered by his son, but this loss was not as great as the loss of Catheryn. Victor did not care for his kingdom that much, he only cared for her. He watched out for her since they were children, and now she was gone, murdered by him, for selfish reasons.

As the last rose pedal caressed the floor, Victor looked up to see a massive demonic figure standing in front of him.

"We have come full circle once again." The demon's voice was like the sound of a thousand souls crying out in pain, raspy and full of confidence.

Victor had never seen such a horrific, terrifying creature. The demon was slightly above seven feet in height. It had an elongated face with small spiked horns protruding from it. The demon had two horns half a foot in length stretched out from each temple. Its skin was a mix of grays and reddish colors, with a pale tone and clammy texture. Victor stayed planted on his knees as he stared up at the demon. Then a familiar sense fell over him. He knew this demon, just not up close and personal. The demon shifted its body and stretched its fingers out as if it was preparing for a fight. Victor just stared blankly at it, lost in his own personal hell, suffering from the loss of everything, and suffering from the guilt that it was him who destroyed his own kingdom.

"Victor, your sins throughout your life grabbed my attention as a means of escaping hell and unleashing it upon the mortal realm once again." The demon began to circle Victor. "In the end, your ultimate sacrifice of your own life paved the way for me to accomplish all this." The demon raised his long toned arm up and pointed to the destruction everywhere. Victor stayed motionless as the demon continued to speak in victory. "For ten of your years, I have had you in this prison, feeding off your tortured soul while only one year in the realm of hell has passed. Your kingdom has remained desecrated and in ruins, for no one dares step foot on this unholy ground." Victor stayed as stiff and ridged as a statue, his eyes, the only thing that moved as the demon continued to circle.

Victor felt his anger and rage build inside him, but felt a helpless feeling of not being able to act upon it. He was still picturing Catheryn in his arms, the rose pedals gliding to the floor, and the warmth he felt when she was alive. But the world was dark and cold, and he was the cause. He felt he needed to do something to prevent the demon from unleashing the realm of hell on the mortal realm.

"There is nothing you can do, Victor. Your time is up, and your soul belongs to me." Victor was about to act as the demon spoke, but another voice grabbed his attention.

"Victor, do not fight back. Your soul can still be saved."

This voice was that of Catheryn's. Victor's rage was about to burst as the loss of her crossed his mind once again. The demon had stopped his movement's right in Victor's point of view. Their eyes met, and Victor made gallant efforts to hold his anger in, but failed to hesitate this time. With a clench of his fist, he felt his sword in hand. He did not question himself as to how it got there; he just lunged forward and slashed the demon across its throat and then drove the blade deep into its chest. "Ah, Victor, you have failed to surprise me once again. Your actions still seem to stay the same, and your misery continues."

The clouds became dark, black as the heart of Satan as the knight entered a forest, riding his noble steed towards a mysterious castle buried deep in the treacherous soul of the haunted forest. This place was deemed, *The Castle of the Dead*. It is known in far off lands that if any man, woman or child dares to enter this forsaken place, their souls shall be tortured and devoured by whatever evil that lays within.

His armor had a faint glow from the beams of light cast through the clouds from the moon as he broke the plain of the forest. The steed which he rode upon was blackish and had chain mail armor with faded symbols marking the kingdom the knight was from. The clouds began to wrap their claws around the moon, casting an eerie liquid shadow upon the land. The glow from the knight's armor faded like a candle smothered with a dark cloth. As the fearless knight slowly stopped near the castle gate, the wind howled like a thousand wolves stalking their prey. The noble steed reared up from this high-pitched howl, knocking its rider to the ground with a hard thud of metal and stone. As his steed ran off, the knight rose to his feet, slightly brushing some of the dirt from his armor, and stood, peering at the castle with a determined look upon his face. He noticed a dark figure in the distance, standing on a destroyed wall of the castle and motioning with his hand for the knight to enter.

Acknowledgments

It was a long journey to make it this far, and I believe this story would never have happened without the support of my family and my friends.

Special thanks to David Salinas, Michael De Jesus, Sandye Noble De Jesus, Alex Arreguin, and my mom. David did an amazing job on the artwork for the book. Mike and Sandye were my editing team. Mr. Arreguin was my literature instructor at Mesa Community College in Arizona, who gave me some great advice on how to progress the story. My mom, for being there every step of the way giving moral support. Last but not least, a special girl named Cat. Thank you for being a part of my life, even if it was for a brief period in time. Thank you, all of you and anyone else not mentioned. Thank you for everything.

About the Author

Jayson Pauley is a new author who lives in Arizona. He is currently a college student studying to master his writing abilities. It has been a wild, and unique journey down this path for him to make it this far, but the path is never-ending. The journey shall continue.